One Elm Books is an imprint of Red Chair Press LLC
www.redchairpress.com

Publisher's Cataloging-In-Publication Data

Names: Blevins, Wiley. | Kissi, Marta, illustrator.

Title: Trevor Lee and the big uh-oh! / by Wiley Blevins ; illustrated by Marta Kissi.

Description: Egremont, Massachusetts : One Elm Books, an imprint of Red Chair Press, [2019]| Summary: "When the new teacher announces all 3rd graders must read in front of everyone on Parents Night, Trevor Lee and his best friend take action before his secret of not being a good reader gets out."

Identifiers: ISBN 9781947159068 (hardcover) | ISBN 9781947159075 (paperback) | ISBN 9781947159082 (ebook)

Subjects: LCSH: Oral reading--Juvenile fiction. | Literacy--Juvenile fiction. | Third grade (Education)--Juvenile fiction. | CYAC: Oral reading--Fiction. | Literacy--Fiction. | Third grade (Education)--Fiction.

Classification: LCC PZ7.B618652 Tr 2019 (print) | LCC PZ7.B618652 (ebook) | DDC [E]--dc23

LC record available at https://lccn.loc.gov/2018946742

Main body text set in 16.5 / 22.5 Minion Pro Regular

Text copyright ©2020 by Wiley Blevins

Copyright © 2020 Red Chair Press LLC

One Elm Books, logo and green leaf colophon are trademarks of Red Chair Press LLC.

519 1P F19FN

TREVOR LEE
AND THE BIG UH-OH!

BY WILEY BLEVINS

ILLUSTRATED BY
MARTA KISSI

ONE ELM
BOOKS

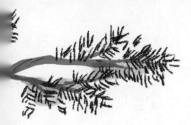

Chapter 1

Putting your underwear on backwards isn't the worst thing that can happen to you on the first day of school. Having everyone find out is.

My name is Trevor Lee McGee. And if there's one thing people know about me it's that school and me don't mix. Like werewolves and vampires. Or peanut butter and pickles. Trust me on that last one.

My grandma, Mamaw McGee, says, "Some days are just bad. You gotta hold your head up high and keep on moving."

Today was going to be one of those days. I could just feel it in my skinny bones. The only skinny thing about me. You see, today was the first day of 3rd Grade.

My best friend Pinky waited for me in front of the school. Well, not exactly in front. He was hiding behind the big pine tree. Near the front door.

Pinky's been my best friend since kindergarten. I know it sounds like a girl's name. But it's not. Pinky's a boy. The kind that picks up frogs and thinks girls smell icky.

Most girls do smell funny, you know. I think they smell like a mix of strawberry and baby butt. Or even noni.

What's noni you ask? Well, it's some weird fruit from the desert. Or is it the rainforest? Maybe it's the moon. I can't remember. Mother bought a whole case of the stuff last summer. Just because she heard on TV it helps you lose weight. It worked. It smelled so gross no one ate it. That's the secret to losing weight. Buy gross food. You'll thank me for that advice when you grow up.

Anyway, back to Pinky. Pinky is not only my best friend, he's the smallest and loudest kid in the class. Pinky says he wants to be a fire truck when he gets older. Or at least as old as my dad. Which is as old as dirt.

I told Mamaw Pinky's great idea about being a fire truck. She just said "Bless his heart" and shook her head.

Mamaw shakes her head a lot when I talk about Pinky. She must have an itchy, itchy brain.

"Psst," said Pinky.

"Why are you hiding behind the tree?" I asked.

"I'm not going in there," he answered.

"Why?"

"Do you know who our teacher is this year?

"No. No idea."

"Miss Booger!"

"Who?"

"Miss Booger. Like the stuff in your nose. My sister had her last year. Says Miss Booger has x-ray vision. Says she can hear your thoughts, too."

"No way!"

"Way."

"And if you talk or even move in class, she… ."

"She what?" I asked moving in closer.

"She gives you the evil stink eye."

"No way!"

"Way."

"Gentlemen," interrupted Principal Harris from the doorway. "Gentlemen!"

"Be very still," Pinky whispered without moving his lips. "If we don't move she won't see us."

"I think that egg has already hatched," I groaned.

Principal Harris was now standing so close I could smell her coffee breath. French roast with milk and two scoops of sugar. I know my morning beverages. Ever since Mother started working, Daddy has me make his morning coffee. Before he'll get out of bed. The lazy butt likes the fancy stuff. It's one of my many new "jobs" since Mother went back to work.

"Gentlemen," she said in a voice too deep for a woman. Or a human. "The bell has rung. You need to find your classroom."

"But…," we both said.

"The only butts I want to hear are yours plopping into chairs."

"Yes, ma'am," I said as we were marched into the school. To face our doom. Our terrifying end. Our death. All at the hands of Miss Booger.

Some days are just bad.

Chapter 2

Miss Booger was a lot prettier and less stinky than I expected.

It turns out her name is actually Miss Burger. Pinky needs to clean out his ears. But, we've decided to call her "The Boog" from here on out. It's easier to talk about your teacher when you use a nickname. Like Mr. Hairy Nose. Or Miss Hair-on-Fire.

The Boog wouldn't let me and Pinky sit beside each other. Something about a story Miss Owens, our 2nd Grade teacher, told her. I had to sit by Sally May. Pinky had to sit by Sally Fay, her twin sister. To say these girls are annoying is like saying dog poo smells. It's a fact.

And it all started only ten minutes after the

bell rang.

"Miss Burger, Miss Burger," Sally May yelled, shaking her hand in the air like a rocket trying to take off. I think that girl has a bad case of the jitters.

"What is it, Sally May?" asked The Boog.

"Miss Burger. Trevor Lee is looking at me."

"That can happen when you have eyes," she answered.

Score one point for The Boog.

"But Miss Burger," Sally May continued. "It ain't right."

Sally Fay, her twin sister, began to jiggle faster than Jell-O in an earthquake.

"Well, I'm sure Trevor Lee is looking because he finds you pretty. Take it as a compliment."

The whole class laughed. Not a giggle. Or a chuckle. Rather, the kind of belly laugh where milk shoots out of your nose.

Minus two points for The Boog.

By the way, Sally May is now my enemy #1. I told her, too. "Sally May. You are my enemy

#1." Just like that. I didn't even care if The Boog heard. Sally May shook her fist at me.

Then Sally Fay shot her hand into the air.

"Miss Burger," she yelled. "Pinky is looking at me."

"Oh brother," The Boog muttered under her breath. She had that scrunched face that teachers get right before they explode. Although not usually on the first day. I grabbed the edge of my desk to get ready for the blow.

"Class. All eyes on the board. All eyes on me. All eyes on your books. For Pete's sake, look at something other than your neighbor!"

"Who's Pete?" I mouthed to Pinky.

"Dunno," he mouthed back with a shrug of his shoulders.

We would have to keep a look out for this Pete guy. Maybe he could join our new club. The Sally May and Sally Fay Are *Sooooooo* Obnoxious Club. Or SMASFASOC for short. It's an exclusive club. I know you'll want to join.

"Children," The Boog went on.

"We will start this morning with reading groups. I want to get a chance to hear all of you read. To show me how much you remember from 2nd Grade."

Pinky shot a look at me. I nodded back.

During the summer we devised a plan for this very moment. You see, I was as good at reading as a fish is good at climbing a cactus.

The plan went something like this: I would first try to get out of reading group. Come up with some big excuse. A real smart one that would trick a teacher. If that didn't work, Pinky would distract the teacher. Like shout "here comes a Martian" or bark like a dog. Then I would sneak out to the bathroom. The teacher wouldn't even know I was gone until reading group was over. Operation Story-Dash was now in effect.

"Okay, children," The Boog announced. "My first reading group will be with Sally May, Sally Fay, Elmer, Pinky, and Trevor Lee. Please come to the table in the back of the room."

Sally May and Sally Fay skipped to the table. Elmer waddled. He wears husky jeans like me. Pinky acted like he was on a Sunday stroll, hands in his pockets. I remained in my seat.

"Trevor Lee," The Boog asked. "Is something wrong?"

"I don't think I can read today, ma'am," I answered. "Cause I have an eye disease."

"An eye disease?"

"Yeah. My doctor says it's... it's... it's dangerous for me to read."

"Dangerous?" asked The Boog.

"Yes. I could go blind or something. And need a white cane with a red tip and a seeing eye dog and a book with those raised dots just to cross the street. You wouldn't want that on your conscience now would you?"

"I'll take my chances," said The Boog. "Join us at the table, Trevor Lee."

I slowly raised myself from the chair. Kinda like if I stood up too fast I'd get dizzy. Then I immediately bent down to tie my shoe. I'm a quick thinker.

"What are you doing now, Trevor Lee?" asked The Boog.

"Well, you wouldn't want me to trip and break my neck now would you?" I asked.

The Boog's face began to twitch.

I think she needs some medicine for that.

The whole class stared as I took baby steps to the table. Foot over foot. Foot over foot. Looking at the ceiling the whole way. Like there was a big spider up there. By the way, someone needs to paint that ceiling. It has tons of brown spots on it. And a couple grizzly-looking dead flies.

"Well," said The Boog. "I've seen a herd of turtles move faster than that. Thank you for joining us, Trevor Lee."

I glanced at Pinky. Clearly we needed to start part 2 of Operation Story-Dash.

"May I sharpen my pencil?" asked Pinky.

"No," answered The Boog.

"May I get a Kleenex?"

"No."

"May I get an eraser? A globe? Brush my teeth?"

"No. No. And no!"

The Boog sure wasn't following the plan. And in a blink of an eye, she handed us our new books. Faster than I can say Mississippi backwards. Well, I can't actually say Mississippi backwards. But if I could, it would be fast.

"Please open your books to page 3," The Boog said.

"Why are we skipping pages 1 and 2?" I asked. "Are those not on the test?"

"We will get to those later, Trevor Lee."

"Oh," I said. "I guess we read out of order in 3rd Grade."

"Would you like to read pages 1 and 2 to the group?" asked The Boog.

"Maybe it's best if we start on page 3," I smiled. "New year, new ways."

The Boog really was a tricky one. It was time for part 3 of Operation Story-Dash. I winked at Pinky to begin and started to shake my legs back and forth. Pinky knew exactly what to do. That's why he's my best friend.

Pinky raised his hand.

"Yes, Pinky," The Boog said with surprise. "Do you want to read?"

"Uh… no," Pinky answered rolling his eyes.

"I just wanted to tell you that Trevor Lee has to pee." I looked up at the ceiling. Again, lots of brown spots. And dead flies.

The Boog stared at Pinky for longer than a teacher should. Then she turned to me.

"If Trevor Lee has to use the restroom," she said, carefully pausing on each word. "Then Mr. Trevor Lee can ask for himself. Besides, we need to learn this story. We're going to read it in front of our moms and dads for Family Night next week."

That did it. The mention of reading in front of a group of people started the flow of pee. Down my leg and onto the floor. In the plan, the pee was pretend. But this sure felt real to me.

Sally May was the first to see it. She screamed and jumped onto her chair.

Sally Fay fainted. That's right. Boom. Face on the floor. I know real fainters fall backwards. I've seen a lot of ladies at church do it. But the big fat faker Sally Fay just laid there like I was fooled. The pee slowly inching toward her.

19

Chapter 3

Lunch couldn't come fast enough. Darlene, the school secretary, gave me a new pair of pants. Two sizes too big. And powder blue. But, the pants covered all the dangling parts.

Lunch was my second favorite time of the school day. I'll tell you about my favorite later.

Pinky raced to the front of the lunch line. I was hot on his heels. The Boog made us march to the back. Something about waiting your turn and walking like 3rd Graders. This 3rd Grade thing wasn't all it was cracked up to be.

I sure could smell the food from where we stood. You know how when someone says chocolate and all you can think about is cake or doughnuts or cookies or ice cream or pie or stuff like that? I bet you're doing it now. Well, that's what I was doing. Pinky kept jabbering about how unfair The Boog was. But, when I looked at him all I saw was a big bologna sandwich. Mamaw says I'm like a dog that way.

"What's it going to be?" asked Pinky. Snapping me out of my food dream.

"Pizza and peas," I announced. "With a side of applesauce." I know my food smells. I can smell a Tic-Tac a mile away. Even with the wind blowing in the opposite direction.

"Rats! I want a hotdog," said Pinky.

"Sorry, buddy. It's pizza and peas."

When we finally got into the kitchen, which took like twenty hundred thousand years, the only pieces of pizza left were the burned ones. The cook behind the counter plopped a droopy slice onto my plate.

"One or two scoops?" she asked, pointing to the peas with her giant metal spoon.

"One, please."

"Nice to see you again this year, Mrs.

Peppercorn," I added.

"So you made it to 3rd Grade?" she asked. "The Lord works in mysterious ways."

"Yes, ma'am," I smiled.

You might think Mrs. Peppercorn was the first lady I've seen with a moustache. You'd be wrong. But she wore it especially well. It matched her husband's.

Then it was Pinky's turn. He and Mrs. Peppercorn had a past. Let's just say it had its ups and downs. Mostly downs.

"One scoop or two?" she asked, glaring at Pinky.

"I'd like a hotdog," Pinky said.

Mrs. Peppercorn tapped the metal spoon on the counter.

And stared.

And stared.

And stared.

"Two scoops it is," she said. "Next!"

The Boog shuffled us out of the line and to our tables.

Pinky just looked at his plate.

"Gobble it down," I told him. "We have work to do. We gotta get me out of Family Night. And we only have a week to do it."

Our plan to get me out of reading group had certainly failed. The Boog was like a puzzle missing one piece. I couldn't quite figure her out yet. We would have to come up with a different plan for Family Night. Something bigger and better.

"So," I said, looking at Pinky. "I'm sure in a pickle with no juice."

"What's the word your daddy uses when your mother tells him he should know what she wants him to do without her telling him?" he asked.

"He says he's *flummoxed*."

"Well, we are close to being completely flummoxed."

"Any ideas?"

"Maybe you can move to a new school."

"Yeah. Right after I fly home from Uranus."

Pinky laughed.

The word *Uranus* always makes Pinky laugh. Like *panties* and Lake *Titicaca*.

"Well, maybe you can tell The Boog you were raised by wolves. That way she wouldn't send home a note about Family Night. Everyone knows wolves can't read."

"If I was raised by wolves," I said, making my "don't be dumb" face. "I'd be hairier. Think, Pinky!"

"Let's just eat," he sighed.

Some days are as
bad as a wolf with no
Red Riding Hood to eat.

Chapter 3½

(That's right. I like fractions.)

At recess, Pinky and I continued to think of ideas to get me out of Family Night. I made a list in my head. And here are our best ones. What do you think?

Ideas for Getting Out of Family Night

1. Run away and join the circus. (Note to self: You're scared of lions and clowns.)

2. Move to Timbuktu and adopt a piglet. (Note to self: Find Timbuktu on a map.)

3. Buy a banjo and become a country music star. (Note to self: Learn how to sing. And play an instrument.)

We ran out of ideas right as the recess bell rang. The Boog lined us up. Then marched us into the classroom. "Like good little soldiers," she said.

Next it was time for math. Finally! Math is the one thing I am good at. It's what keeps me from jumping out the window every time The Boog turns her back. That and the fact we're on the 3rd floor of the school building.

The Boog passed out our new math books. The kind you can't write in. Unlike in 2nd Grade. Then she stood very still at the front of the room. And smiled. Like an ice cube with teeth.

"I have a surprise for you," she said. " I hear you all worked so hard in 2nd Grade. To learn how to add and subtract—all the basics. As a result, this year in math we will be focusing on something very grown-up. Word problems. Real life ways to use the math you have learned."

"Say what?" I mumbled under my breath. "Does The Boog have moonshine in her Kool-Aid?" I couldn't have been more shocked if she would have let a stinker after every sentence.

Math is NOT, and I repeat, NOT about words. It's about numbers. 1, 2, 38, and everything in between. Word problems are like a big bowl of liver and spinach. They might be good for you. But you wouldn't touch them with a ten-foot pole. Ten foot... now that's real-life math.

"Okay... well... let me give you an example," said The Boog. Cause we were all staring at her like she had three heads. Two big ones and a little one with curly hair. "Let's do a problem using fractions, since we will be learning a lot more about them this year." Then she wrote one of those wordy word problems on the board.

"Lets read the problem together," she said. "1, 2, Ready? Read."

> If a pie has 8 slices and my friend eats
> ½ the pie. What will I get?

Everyone started reading out loud. Except me. I just moved my lips up and down. Like a horse eating peanut butter. Unfortunately, when everyone stopped my lips kept moving. I wasn't what you would call "paying close attention."

"Are you chewing gum, Trevor Lee?" asked The Boog.

"No ma'am," I said.

"Then what's in your mouth?"

"I think a dead fly from the ceiling fell into it, ma'am."

"Gross!" yelled Sally May and Sally Fay.

"Tastes like chicken," I said. And licked my lips.

"Well, just swallow whatever it is," said The Boog. "Do you need to read the word problem again?"

"No, ma'am," I lied.

"So," said The Boog, "If my friend eats half of this pie, what will I get?"

"A belly ache," blurted out Pinky. "That is if you eat what's left."

"That might be true," said The Boog. "But next time raise your hand. Anyone else? How many pieces of pie will I get to eat? Sally May?"

"My mother doesn't let us eat pie, ma'am. She says if you eat a lot of pie, you'll get fat."

"Or the runs," piped in Sally Fay.

Everyone nodded in agreement.

The Boog stomped her foot to stop our nodding. Then she yelled, "FOUR! I will get to eat four small slices of pie. Sugar-free. Organic. Low-calorie. Mother-approved. Fruit pie."

Then she drew on the board. She said it was a pie. But it just looked like a lousy circle. And divided the circle-pie into eight slices. She asked Elmer to color in four of the slices. He complained it made him hungry. Finally, she asked us to count the slices not colored in. And she was right. There were four crumby slices left. I wondered if she would share them with us.

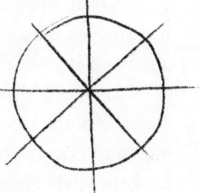

"See," she said. "Fractions are as easy as pie." Then she laughed at her own joke.

We stared in silence.

"Well, now it's your turn," she said. Then closed her eyes and took a deep breath. Clearly glad the lesson was over.

The Boog handed each of us a page with five word problems on it. There were more sentences on this page than out-of-control kids on Halloween. What was I going to do?

I looked at the first problem. Then glanced over at Pinky. He wasn't having a lick of trouble. In fact, everyone looked like they were enjoying these wordy problems. Impossible! I felt like I had stepped onto Pluto. Which isn't even a planet anymore. If you can imagine that.

So, I went back to problem #1. I recognized a couple of the words. And crossed my fingers, toes, and eyes the rest weren't important. Unfortunately, the words I did know didn't give me enough clues. So, I decided to just add up all the numbers I saw, then divide in half. I spotted a 5, a 2, and a 3. That added up to 10. ½ of 10 was easy. 5. I scribbled 5 on my paper. As Mamaw always says, "There's more than one way to wash a stinky dog."

As I started problem #2, everyone around me began handing in their papers.

And then there it was. The most beautiful sound in the world. Better than a chorus of angels from heaven above. The end-of-the-day bell. My most favorite time of the day.

You'd think I'd be more excited. Especially since it's my most favorite time of day. But, I wasn't. Cause I still hadn't decided on a plan. I had four more wordy problems to do. And The Boog was trying to destroy my love of the one thing worth coming to school for. Math. She was a one-woman, pink-lipped, sort-of-nice-smelling wrecking ball.

"What do I do now?" I asked Pinky.

"About what?

"About Family Night!" I said.

"Let's sleep on it," said Pinky. "Maybe the answer will come in a dream. I heard on TV people can solve their problems in their sleep.

Unless they're snoring."

"The only dreams I have are of cows with polka dots chasing me in the field behind our barn," I sighed.

"Oh, right," said Pinky. "And those always end with you not drinking milk for a week."

"Speaking of cows… it's my turn to feed the chickens tonight. You know what that means."

"Hippie?"

"Yeah. Hippie the Rooster. The evil ninja rooster out to destroy the world. One peck at my heels at a time."

Life on a farm sure isn't easy. Ever since Mother and Daddy got so busy, it's been even worse. I'm beginning to think the only reason they had me is to do their work. To make coffee. To clean the house. To feed the chickens. To pull the weeds in the garden. Anything they don't want to do.

"Good luck with that," Pinky said and shook his head.

"What an interesting first day," The Boog interrupted as we lined up to go home. "See ya tomorrow, Trevor Lee," she smiled.

"I'll discuss that with my parents," I warned. And marched straight out the door.

Some days are
worse than a pie
made of toenails.

Chapter 4

Mamaw was waiting for me at home. She has lived with us ever since Papaw passed away. Which is very different from passing a ball or passing gas. Although he did both of those really well, too.

"So, did you learn anything today?" Mamaw asked as she hugged me.

Mamaw hugs so hard I can't hardly breathe. She says it's so I can feel the love deep inside.

"I don't think this 3rd Grade thing is gonna work out," I answered. "Maybe I should be like home-schooled, but without the schooled. What was 3rd Grade like for you?"

"3rd Grade?" asked Mamaw. "Why Trevor Lee, I'm as old as the mountains. With these cobwebs in my brain, I can't even remember yesterday."

Mamaw liked to talk about school about as much as I did. In fact, I didn't think I had ever heard her talk about it.

"What's the problem, sweetpea?" she asked.

"Well, it's these doggone long words when I try to read. They're Enemy #2."

"Enemy #2?" Mamaw asked.

"Yeah, well, Sally May is Enemy #1," I explained. Mamaw shook her head like she understood.

"Heck, the short words aren't that friendly either. It don't make no sense. How come the letters *ea* in *heat* say "eeeee," but in the word *head* they say "eh." Who made up that rule? A drunk turtle?"

"Oh dear," sighed Mamaw.

I put my head in my hands. "All this talk about reading has made me hungrier than a pig on a diet."

"Well, here's a biscuit for ya. It'll hold you over until dinner," said Mamaw. "Your mother and daddy will be home late again. Just us two little birds here."

"That reminds me," I said. "Time to feed the chickens."

"Now you stand up to that old rooster. You hear me?"

Standing up wasn't exactly what I had in mind. I had a Stop, Drop, and Roll plan that I was working on. Like when there's a big fire and the fireman's ladder can't reach you.

First I tiptoe as close to the chicken coop as I can get. When Hippie the Rooster spies me I freeze. Like a cherry Popsicle. Or a banana one. I like those, too.

Then I drop to the ground. So low I blend in with the grass. Like the bugs and worms. Careful not to eat any, though.

After that I roll to the chicken coop door. Hippie will just think I'm a tumbleweed. And pay no attention to me.

Finally, I jump up and dash into the coop, feed the chickens, then dash back to the house. It will help if I scream all the way back. Makes me run faster.

"Okay you ninja rooster," I whispered. "Today I am king of the chicken coop."

I tiptoed close to the coop. Careful not to make a sound.

Just as Hippie spotted me, I stopped. "What next? Oh, yeah. Drop, Trevor Lee. Drop!"

I dropped to the ground. Hippie's evil head twisted back and forth. And back and forth. And then back. But not forth.

Now time to roll. Side over side. Side over side. Side over… ouch!… side. I hadn't planned on all the little pebbles along the way. I would have more dents in me than my Uncle Lum's old truck when this was over.

Suddenly, I felt something that wasn't quite a pebble.

A peck!

And then another one. And another one. Hippie was on top of me. That crazy bird was attacking me.

I screamed and rolled. And screamed and rolled. And screamed some more. Kinda like a girl. But only higher. Since we're friends I can trust you with that secret. Right?

Well, Hippie was fired up. His wings flapped as fast as my arms flopped.

I rolled with him on top of me until I rolled into the coop door.

"Today I am king of the coop," I yelled through flapping wings. Then I sat up. Hippie now doing a rooster dance on my head. "Grab the coop door," I reminded myself. "But open your eyes first, Trevor Lee."

It helps when you talk to yourself in situations like these. No need to thank me for that advice.

I did finally get the coop door open, swatted off Hippie, and slipped inside. Slamming the door shut.

"I am king of the coop," I crowed. My voice a bit crackly.

Hippie pecked at the door. Like an out-of-control jackhammer on high.

I turned around to face the hens. One hen laid half a dozen eggs in all the excitement. A few others ran to the back of the coop and squawked nervously. I could swear a couple rolled their eyes at me.

So I did it. Mission accomplished.

But… uh… oh. There was one big problem. The chicken's food was in a barrel.

Outside the coop.

And there was no way I was going to leave this chicken coop. Not until Hippie left. And the way he was kicking up dirt outside the door, he could stay there until Christmas. In the year 3000.

I had twenty hungry hens eyeing me. And one angry rooster blocking me in.

On a scale of 1 to 10.
With 1 being BAD.
And 10 being DISASTER.
Some days are a 72½.

Chapter 4½

Once back in the house, Mamaw tried to cheer me up. By playing "He-Man of the World." We started by doing push-ups. Mamaw got down on her knees. Like she was ready to say a prayer. And stuffed her dress between her legs.

"A He-Man can still be a lady," she explained.

Then down-up, down-up, down-up. She finished three red-faced, grunt-filled push-ups.

I flopped down on the floor and did 3½. I didn't want to show her up too bad. Plus I was a bit tired from my Hippie run-in.

The next round of the competition involved lifting. The heaviest thing in the room. Since that was Mamaw, we agreed to lift something more manageable. Barks-a-Lot, our stinky hound dog.

He barely broke his snore as we took turns lifting him on and off the couch.

We were about to get started with the next round of the competition. Karate kicks. When I heard the car door slam. Mother was home. A few minutes later I heard Daddy pull in the driveway.

"How was your first day of school?" Mother asked. As she put down the bags of groceries.

"Okay."

"What did you learn?" asked Daddy. Right behind her with another armful of groceries.

"Nothing."

"You mean to tell me you spent all day at that there school and all you learned was nothing?" Daddy asked.

"I don't know."

"Well, who's your teacher this year?" asked Mother.

"Miss Burger."

"Oh that must be Dr. Burger's daughter, Sunny," said Daddy.

"Sunny Burger?" I asked. "Sounds like a

breakfast sandwich at McDonald's. I'll have a Sunny Burger. Hold the pickle."

Mamaw giggled so hard she snorted.

"I hear she's real pretty," said Daddy.

"Whatever."

"Do you have homework?" asked Mother.

"No."

"No learning and no homework," said Daddy. "Did you really go to school today, Trevor Lee? Or did you and Pinky go fishing?"

Fishing. Why hadn't I thought of that?

"I'm not feeling so well," I answered. "May I go to my room?"

"Yes, honey," said Mamaw. "I'll call you down when supper's ready."

I ran upstairs to my room. Just as I shut the door, I heard Mamaw say my name through the vent. Sounds from the kitchen rise up through it and into my room. If I lean my ear right next to it, I can hear whatever Mamaw, Mother, and Daddy say in the kitchen. Even if they're whispering. It's how I almost always find out my birthday present before the big day.

"Was it that bad?" asked Daddy.

"He didn't give any details," said Mamaw. "But when he got home he looked like a cat with no meow. "

"I wonder if it's the reading thing again. I thought the help he got this past summer would get him caught up," said Daddy. "Have you heard him read lately?"

"No," said Mother. "I barely had time to buy his new school clothes."

"Well, what are we gonna do?" asked Daddy.

"We can't afford to pay for a tutor," said Mother. "Maybe we should talk to Miss Burger. See if he needs to go back to 2nd Grade."

I slammed the vent shut. I had heard enough.

The thought of leaving 3rd Grade. Without Pinky. Well, it was just too much. I crawled into bed. And put the covers over my head.

Chapter 5

"What happened to your face?" asked Pinky the next day at school.

"Hippie."

"So the plan worked?"

"Not exactly. Mamaw had to rescue me. It took a big broom and a little cussin'."

The Boog's eyes got real big when she saw me, too. Like a monkey at the zoo. The ones with the puffy red butts.

"Welcome back, Trevor Lee," she smiled.

I gave her the face.

It looked something like this.

"I hope those scratches clear up before Monday," she said.

"Why Monday?"

I shouldn't have asked.

"'Cause Monday is Picture Day," The Boog answered. "These are the pictures we'll be showing on Family Night."

Pinky grabbed his head.

Last year Pinky's mom had what his dad called a "hairy-brained" idea the day before Picture Day. To give Pinky a perm. She always did the same with Pinky's sisters.

Well, the perm didn't quite take. But the picture sure was taken.

I had to help Pinky to his desk as he was a bit shaken by the news.

"Please sit, children. We have a special day today," announced The Boog.

Now this can't be good. *Special* is teacher code for "boring."

"Today I will assign my special helpers for the week."

See.

Big whoop.

"And, I will assign the parts each of you will read on Family Night."

No she didn't.

"Excuse me," I said, raising my hand. "My parents can't come to Family Night, so I won't need a part. Thank you anyway, ma'am."

"I didn't send home a letter about Family Night yet, Trevor Lee," said The Boog. "So how do you know your parents are busy?"

"I told them all about it," I answered. I'm a quick thinker.

"And what night next week did you tell them Family Night is taking place?" asked The Boog.

"Uh... ."

The Boog hadn't actually shared that piece of information with us. Think, Trevor Lee. Think fast!

"I told them it was probably every night, ma'am. And they said, 'Oops. Sorry.'"

The Boog walked toward me. Her shoes

clicking on the floor. Like a giant cockroach in heels.

"Every child in this class will be reading a part for Family Night," stated The Boog. "Including you."

And then she did it. She pointed at me. Even I know that's rude.

The Boog went on to explain what we would be doing over the next two weeks to prepare for Family Night. In addition to taking class pictures, we would be going on a field trip and doing some *interesting* writing about it. "Interesting" was her word. Not mine. All of these things would be shown on Family Night as an example of what we are learning and the "wonderful experiences" we are having in 3rd Grade. Again, her words. Not mine. She emphasized that we were to put our best foot forward. To make a good impression as the year began.

Since Mamaw says I have two left feet, I guess it doesn't matter which foot I put forward. Or backwards. Or slide side-to-side. So I ignored her last comment about the feet.

Then she put a checklist on the board. To show all the things we would need to accomplish before Family Night.

"It helps to make a list," The Boog said. "You set a goal, then divide it into smaller tasks along the way. It makes it easier for you to reach your goal. Plus it's a lot of fun to check off each task as you finish it. Gives you real satisfaction!" And she swept her arms in the air like she was hugging a ghost floating above her.

I shot one of my looks at Pinky. And twisted my finger around my ear. The international symbol for crazy.

Then The Boog went on. "Each of you will have special jobs to do this week and throughout the year," she explained.

After that, The Boog introduced the Helper of the Week board. And pointed at me. Since my name was on the Helper board.

Again, rude.

I would have to write the governor about this.

Or maybe the President of the United States of the Americas. Do you have his address?

Anyway… So, I bet you're wondering who got these so-called "special" jobs?

Sally May got to take the attendance slip to the office and read the morning announcements.

"It's cause I'm the teacher's favorite," she stood up and declared. The Boog told her to sit down.

Sally Fay looked like she was gonna cry.

Elmer got to clean the board.

He's good with simple tasks.

Bobby Sue got to lead the recess and lunch lines. She's the tallest in the class.

Pinky got nothing.

Walter got nothing.

Brandy, Penelope, Bo, and the rest of the class. Nothing.

But feeding the hamster. Giving it water. Cleaning out its cage. Of hamster poo. And hamster throw-up. And other gross hamster stuff. That went to none other than…

Trevor Lee.

HELPER BOARD

Sally May · · · · ATTENDANCE
Elmer · · · · · · CLEAN THE BOARD
Bobby Sue · · · · RECESS LEADER
Trevor Lee · · · HAMSTER HELPER

That's me.

Now let me tell you, there's another important thing everyone knows about me. Even more than I hate school, I hate rats. I have an *I hate rats* t-shirt. *I hate rats* baseball cap. *I hate rats* underwear with *I* on the front and *hate rats* on the back. One word per cheek. That's the same underwear I wore backwards last year on the first day of school.

And a hamster is nothing more than a hairy rat. Like my Uncle Lum. At least that's what my mother calls him. But not when my daddy can hear.

"Excuse me, ma'am," I said. "When does this rat cleaning begin?"

"Now, Trevor Lee. And every morning this week."

"Well, at least I don't have to read to do this job," I mumbled under my breath. And scooted over to the cage.

So here I am. Me and that hairy rat.

No, not my Uncle Lum.

The hamster.

Of course, no one told me how to feed, water, and clean the cage of a hamster. I think that's like child neglect or something. I should report it to the authorities.

Then I spotted a blue index card. Taped to the outside of the cage. This just might be the cleaning directions. Only I couldn't read them. I could, however, make out a few words. *It. The.*

Pick up. Top. And *Back.* Based on that, I had an idea of what to do.

"Hurry up, Trevor Lee," said The Boog. "A good helper is a fast helper."

Okay...

So, not only did I have to clean this nasty hamster cage, I had to do it like I had a motor attached to my be-hind.

I held my nose with one hand and lifted the cage door with the other. The hamster scurried under the cedar shavings.

"Come on, you nasty rat," I whispered.

He peeked one eye out from under the shavings.

And showed his teeth.

Like an evil Easter Bunny.

I had to get him out of the cage to clean it. Even I knew that.

So, I slowly put my hand—the one formerly holding my nose and saving me from stink injury—inside the cage. There are probably a trillion million billion gazillion germs in there. I

could die of some tropical disease like swamp rat fever or something. That sure would teach The Boog.

Next I tiptoed over to the hamster with my fingers.

I then carefully raised my hand. It was above the hamster like an umbrella in a hurricane.

Now it was time to touch the hamster.

I mean, really folks. Who forces a child to touch a hairy rat?

With one quick swoop and a little squeak (from me, not the hamster) I grabbed it.

He wiggled inside my hand.

Like a hairy worm.

There was no way I could clean the cage with the other hand.

Where could I put this hamster?

I looked to the right. I looked to the left. I looked up. I looked down. I even did the hokey pokey and turned myself around. No safe place to put that hamster.

Then I had a genius idea.

Plop. Down went the hamster.

Now I could focus on the job of a Hamster Helper. After all, that was my "special" job.

I decided I could do it in four easy steps.

Step 1: Clean the cage.
Gross, but done.

Step 2: Add food.
Done.

Step 3: Give fresh water.
Done. Done. And done.

Step 4: Get the hamster back into the cage.
Easy, but there was one issue. A big one. I

couldn't quite remember where I put the hamster.

Think, Trevor Lee. Think!

Oh, right. It is...

"Miss Burger," yelled Sally May. "Trevor Lee has a hamster on his head."

"Trevor Lee!" The Boog shouted.

Just as she did, the hamster woke up from its nap in my hairy-head nest. And dove off.

I chased after it.

Sally May jumped onto her chair. And screamed some more.

Sally Fay fake fainted. Boom. Face down on the floor. I swear that girl spends more time on the ground than dirt. She really needs to get a grip.

I ran some more until Pinky stopped me. Cause I was just running in circles. Yelling "Calm down everyone. I got this under control. No need to call the cops."

"Buddy," said Pinky. "You have a bigger problem than a runaway hamster. You have *hmmm-hmmm* in your hair."

"I have what in my hair?"

"*Hmmm... hmmmm.*"

"You got hamster poo in your hair!" yelled
Sally May as she covered her face with her hands.

Some days are like a big,
red rash right where
you don't want it.

Chapter 6

After recess there was one less helper on the Helper Board. Me.

I would remember to forget to tell Mother and Daddy about this. And unless Pinky and I could come up with a plan to get me out of Family Night, there was a chance The Boog might tell 'em. She's sneaky that way. I can tell.

Darlene, the school secretary, washed out my hair and I was back in class. Just in time for The Boog to hand out our reading parts for Family Night.

We were going to read "The Little Red Hen." I knew the story. We read it in 1st Grade. But this was one of those wacky retellings. The one in which the Little Red Hen's friends get a lawyer.

And sue her for not giving them any of the bread she made.

The Little Red Hen and Her Lazy-Butt Friends

Once upon a time, the little red hen decided to make some yummy bread. To eat with her yummy tomato soup. "There's nothing better than some piping-hot fresh bread," she thought.

To begin, the little red needed to gather the wheat. So, she asked her friends for help.

"Who will help me gather the wheat?" she asked. "I know it's a bit tiresome, but I could surely use the help."

"Not I," said the lazy dog.

"Not I," said the lazy cat.

"Not I," said the lazy pig.

So the little red hen gathered the wheat. All by herself.

Next, the little red hen needed to thresh the wheat. She asked the three little pigs for help. "Who will help me thresh the wheat?" she asked. "Beating the wheat can be a lot of fun. And it's great exercise," she said.

"Not I," said the pig with straw.

"Not I," said the pig with sticks.

"Not I," said the pig with bricks.

So the little red hen threshed the wheat. All by herself.

After that, the little red hen had to knead the bread dough. She asked Cinderella for help. "Who will help me knead the bread dough?" she asked. "It's a lot more enjoyable than sweeping chimney dust.

"Not I," said Cinderella. "I have a ball to go to. And pretty glass slippers to polish."

So the little red hen kneaded the bread dough. All by herself.

Then, it was time for the little red hen to bake the bread. She asked Jack and Jill for help. "Who will help me bake the bread?" she asked. "It's really an easy task, but I could use the company.

"Not I," said Jack.

"Not I," said Jill.

"We have to run up a hill. And fetch a pail of water."

So the little red hen baked the bread. All by herself.

Finally, it was time to eat the little red hen's bread.
"Who will help me eat this yummy, piping-hot bread?"
asked the little red hen.

"I will," said her lazy friends.

"I will," said the three little pigs.

"I will," said Cinderella.

"I will," said Jack and Jill.

"Well, you did not help me make the bread," said the little red hen. So I will eat it. All of it."

"ALL... BY... MY... SELF."

And that's just what she did. Until the big, bad wolf showed up! "We'll sue you," shouted the little red hen's lazy friends.

You see, the lazy friends had hired the big, bad wolf—the best and most crooked lawyer in the land— to force the little red hen to give them some of the bread.

But it was too late. The big bad wolf had already eaten the bread. And drank the soup. He said it was his lawyer fee.

So, the little red hen's lazy-butt friends all went to bed. Hungry.

THE END

So about those parts for Family Night.

Walter is the best reader in our class. So, he was assigned the whole first page to read.

Sally May and Sally Fay asked if they could read together. They dress alike. Talk alike. Probably even snore alike. So, The Boog said "yes."

Pinky, Elmer, Brandy, Penelope, Bo, and the rest of the class each got a paragraph. A whole paragraph.

That's like three or four long sentences. There is no way I could read that much.

Then it was my turn.

"I have the most important page for you to read, Trevor Lee," said The Boog. "The last page."

I gulped.

I saw how long the first page was. I could only imagine how many words were on the last page. That's like the end of the story. When everything happens.

"Pinky," I said. "I can't bear to look. You look and tell me what it says."

Pinky flipped to the end of the story. In big letters it read "THE END."

Some days do get better, like when your Mamaw surprises you with ice cream for supper.

Chapter 7

After assigning our parts, The Boog called each of us over to the reading table. One student at a time. To practice for Family Night and to reread to her one of the books we were supposed to read over the summer. She said it was a reading assessment. Whatever. I guess she was too lazy to read it herself.

"I already read this," I told her when she handed me the book. I fibbed. Which is not the same as a full-out lie if you tell it to save your little be-hind from terror, torture, or any other T-word. Like T-Rex. "I don't want to bore you again with the same old story. Maybe I could just tell you a story?"

"I like listening to all my students read, Trevor

Lee," The Boog said. I stared at her nose waiting for it to grow. Like Pinocchio's. From the big lie she just told.

I looked down at the page. And stared at it.

I saw lots of long words. I've had this fear of long words every since 1st Grade. I didn't think a word should ever be longer than three or four letters. Like *cat*. Or *ick*. Or *duh*. It was when words got all fat that reading got hard. I think there ought to be a law: No words bigger than *butt*. Unless it's your name, of course.

"Don't you think it's a bit warm in here to read?" I asked. And fanned my face like it was July.

"Put your finger on the first word," she said. Ignoring me.

I did.

My fingernail had some dirt under it. So I picked at it. Then I tapped on the word. I wiggled my finger around the word. I stared at the picture praying it would reveal the word. And I waited.

"Focus," The Boog said. "Tell me the first

sound in the word."

"I've never heard it make a sound, ma'am," I said. "If it could talk this reading thing wouldn't be so hard."

"Let's do it together then," she said. "The letter 'g' makes the "guh" sound."

"Like you're guzzling grape juice," I said. "Guh, guh, guh." I pretended to drink a big glass of the purple stuff.

"And these two oo's together make the "ew" sound," The Boog added.

"Like you just caught Sally May out of her seat. Ewww Sally May, you're in trouble!" I laughed.

Sally May turned around and stuck her tongue out at me. But The Boog didn't see it.

"That's right," The Boog nodded. "Now try sounding out the whole word."

"Guh, guh, gewwws. Goose?" I asked.

"Perfect!" The Boog smiled.

We continued on through the rest of the words in the sentence. I could tell The Boog was as flat out exhausted as I was when I got to the end. So she let me escape back to my desk.

Just in time for math. No, not numbers math. Wordy math. Or what Pinky calls "when math went wrong." Even though he's good at it. That's why he's my best friend.

The Boog had already written three wordy problems on the board.

"Read the problems carefully," she said. "Like a number detective. Then write your answer on a piece of paper. But remember… you must write a number AND a word. You can't just write the number 4. You have to tell me 4 *what*, like 4 apples or 4 bears. Everyone understand?"

We all nodded whether we understood or not. It's the quickest way to shut a teacher up.

So, here's the first problem:

4 kids each get 2 apples. They eat ½ of their apples. How many were eaten?

I looked at the words. I only recognized kids and get. So, I went to my back-up plan. I added up all the numbers. That was easy. 4 plus 2 equals

6. Then I divided in ½. And wrote my answer.

3 kids

I was sure I got it right. I was a math wizard, after all. I was so sure I did something I hadn't done all year yet.

I raised my hand.

"Yes, Trevor Lee," The Boog said in a surprised, high-pitched way. "You want to answer #1?"

"Yes ma'am," I smiled confidently. "It's 3 kids."

Everyone giggled.

Except Pinky.

"I think you might have misread the problem," said The Boog. And hushed the class with one of her stink eye looks.

Then she read aloud the problem.

How many were eaten?

3 kids

I buried my face in the palm of my hand. How had math so quickly become the worst part of my day?

We spent the rest of the day getting ready for our Apple Picking Field Trip. And me recovering from my math horror.

The Boog pointed to our checklist of Family Night preparation steps. To help us remember what we needed to do. And "feel good" about completing another task toward accomplishing our goal. It wasn't my goal. So I didn't really care. But it sure got The Boog all worked up. Teachers like to repeat the same nonsense (I mean "information") over and over and over. Until you start hearing it in your dreams. I guess they teach them that in teacher school. Or the principal makes them do it. Maybe old people are just real forgetful.

Then The Boog passed out small apple cut-outs. Made from red construction paper. She asked us to write a word on our apple that could describe an apple.

"Remember," she said. "Your parents will read these on Family Night."

There she goes on about that Family Night. The Boog just can't give it a rest.

It seems that our work will be on display all over the classroom for Family Night. Along with photos from our field trip. Pictures of me holding an apple. Me biting an apple. Me in an apple bubble bath. Or something like that.

"We'll hang these under a sign that reads 3rd Grade GREATS," she announced. "Our class slogan!" And she held her hands in the air again. Like she had just won a race.

"Should be 3rd Grade GREATS Stink,"

I whispered to Pinky.

"Or, 3rd Grade GREATS Stink Like Sally May's breath," whispered back Pinky.

"Or, 3rd Grade GREATS Stink Like Sally Fay's Feet," I laughed.

"Trevor Lee," interrupted The Boog. "Do you have a comment?"

"Love the class slogan," I smiled and put my two thumbs up. I'm a quick thinker.

Pinky put his two thumbs up, too. That's why he's my best friend.

"Wonderful," said The Boog.

I think she bought it.

"But you'll get more writing done, Trevor Lee, when your hand is moving. Instead of your mouth."

She has a point.

The Boog then walked around the room and read what everyone put on their apples.

Walter wrote "scrumptious." That kid is a brain.

Sally May and Sally Fay both wrote "delishus."

The Boog said they spelled it wrong. She wrote what she said was the correct spelling on the board:

D-E-L-I-C-I-O-U-S

That sure didn't look right to me. Note to self: Check to see if The Boog really went to college.

On my apple, I wrote "red." It was one of the few words I knew I could spell right. And drew a worm with a smiley face. Sally May said it was gross. So, Pinky drew a worm on his apple, too. That's another reason why he's my best friend.

Sally Fay took one look at it and started to spin. Like she was going to faint. But she held on this time.

Then we had to write color poems. Don't ask me why. It was on the list.

Walter wrote:

Summer is... red.

Blazing sun, beach-burned shoulders and cheeks, the lifeguard's trunks.

Wild strawberry, Mars red, scarlet, and razzmatazz.

That kid is a show-off.
Sally May and Sally Fay wrote:

Orange.

Orange is like pumpkins, squash, and Bobby Sue's hair.

Orange dresses, orange shoes, and orange crayons.

Those two aren't very creative.
I chose the color white. I wrote:

White.
White is like chicken poop.

The Boog read it and said it was "short and sweet." I think she really liked it. Sally May looked jealous. I don't care cause she's still my enemy #1.
Then The Boog gave each of us a slip of paper. It had instructions on it for our field trip.

Instructions is just a fancy word teachers use to mean "lots of stupid rules."

Luckily, there were only three. And she read them aloud to us.

1. *No throwing, biting, or smashing apples.*
   How were we going to have fun?

2. *No climbing ladders. Only pick up apples from the ground.*
   Sally Fay the fake fainter would be good at that. She liked being on the floor.

3. *Stay with your field trip partner at all times.*
   This was an easy one. Pinky was stuck to me like a tongue on a flagpole in the middle of winter. Pinky knew a lot about that. Principal Harris wouldn't let him anywhere near a flag from October through May.

Maybe this field trip would turn out okay after all.

Some days end almost right.
Almost.

Chapter 7¾

Mamaw lay sleeping on the couch when I got home. She sometimes falls asleep watching her afternoon shows. Especially if they're reruns. She says watching the same show twice is like washing your hair, then running out in a rainstorm without a hat.

I grabbed a snack from the kitchen. Then sat and waited for her to come back to life. The worse thing you can do is wake a sleeping grandma. They tend to swing their arms.

Barks-a-Lot curled up next to Mamaw. And started whining for a little of my snack. I don't know if it was Barks-a-Lot whining and licking Mamaw's face or me laughing that woke her up.

"Sleeping your life away, Mamaw? I asked.

"Oh dear," she mumbled. "Is it that time already? I have far too much to do before your Mother and Daddy get home. I can't be glued to this couch all day." With that Mamaw rolled on her side. And swung her legs onto the floor. This caused her to spin and flip upright. Then she pushed with all her might to stand. I grabbed her shoulders and pulled.

"That'll about do it," she said. Now standing. And swayed a bit from side to side as she caught her balance. "So," she went on, "good day or bad day?"

"I'm sitting on the fence with this one," I said.

"Speaking of fences, I need to pick some fruit from the back of the field. Wanna join me?"

I loved walking to the edge of our farm. Hugging the fence was a line of fruit trees. Apples. Peaches. Pears. And Plums. There were even a few grape vines weaving in and out of the fence. It was like our very own fruit stand.

It took us a while to get there. We had to pass the chicken coop without the chickens seeing us and squawking for food. We also had to pass the barn, unlatch the fence gate without any cows escaping, and watch our step as we made our way to the back of the field. We didn't want to get anything unexpected on our shoes. The cows graze and run in the field. But it's also their bathroom.

Once under the trees, we filled one large bag with apples and two smaller bags with peaches. We didn't have enough grapes to fill a bag so we just plucked a few handfuls.

"So, why are you sitting on the fence about school?" asked Mamaw. As we sat for a spell

under one of the apple trees. Mamaw pulled out a chocolate bar hidden in her dress pocket. Split it in ½. Almost. And gave me the slightly bigger piece.

I told Mamaw all about word problems, the Family Night reading, and how I didn't want to go back to 2nd Grade.

Mamaw pulled me in close. And wrapped her arm around me.

"Let me tell you a secret," she said. "When your Daddy was about your age, he and school had a terrible battle, too. He came home every day with his chin dragging on the floor. One day he announced, 'I ain't goin' back.' Me and your Papaw marched down to the school to see what was the matter."

"What was wrong?" I asked.

"Turns out, your Daddy was having a devil of a time with multiplication."

"Really?" I asked. "But math is so easy! At least the kind with numbers is."

"Not for your Daddy," said Mamaw.

"What happened next?"

"Your Papaw worked with him on his homework. The teacher gave him extra lessons before and after school. I said a prayer or two. And after a while, a long while, he did better. He was able to make it through. But he never did take a real liking to it. Always said math was like a relative you hated to see come visit. You had to sit through it, but you didn't have to enjoy it."

"Do you think the same thing can happen to me?" I asked. "With reading?"

"I'm as sure as the sun rising in the morning," Mamaw said with a smile. And I knew she believed it.

"You never do talk about when you were in school. Why Mamaw?"

"Ain't much to tell," she answered softly. Then got quiet.

"Well, look at the time. We best be getting a move on. We need to feed those chickens or they'll refuse to lay us eggs," she finally said.

With that we gathered our bags of fruit. And

headed back.

"I'll race you to the chicken coop," I laughed. And took off running. I ran all the way to the edge of the field, near the gate. I was about to unlatch it when I spotted Hippie. And Hippie spotted me. Luckily, when he saw Mamaw puffing and panting behind me, he high-tailed it in the opposite direction. He ran as scared as a pig at a pork roast.

I swung open the coop door. The chickens greeted us with a squawk fest. And Mamaw greeted the chickens by name.

"Hello, Mabel. Hello, Ethel. Hello Edith-Ann. Yes, I see you too Veronica."

"Veronica?" I asked.

"Yeah," said Mamaw. "She's the one that flirts with the rooster. See how the other hens keep their eye on her?"

Veronica strutted in front of the nests. Then poked her head out the coop door. Like she was looking for Hippie.

"Get back in here girl," Mamaw said as she

swatted her tail. Then poured the chickens some fresh water from the hose. While I scooped out some chicken feed from the barrel. Something tasty for them to munch on. We were almost finished when we heard the car doors.

Mother and Daddy were home.

"Now don't go telling your Daddy that story I told you," Mamaw reminded me.

"My lips are sealed with super-glue. And duct tape on top of that," I said.

Mamaw put her arm around me as we walked back to the house.

We took off our dirty shoes at the door. Also by the door rested my bookbag. The crumpled field trip permission slip poking out.

I was so happy about Mamaw's secret, I decided to deal with that later.

Some days end just fine.
Unless you forget to do
something important.

Chapter 8

Now everyone knows you can't go on a field trip unless you have one important thing. A signed permission slip.

Mother and Daddy flat-out failed to sign my slip. Well, maybe they didn't hear me ask them. Before they went to bed. Or left for work.

Or, maybe I just plain forgot. The details aren't that important now. Since it clearly is not, and I repeat "not," my fault.

So, it was up to Mamaw.

"Can you read this and sign it?" I asked. "It's kinda important."

Mamaw picked up the paper. Upside-down. Stared at it for a second, then handed it back to me.

"Trevor Lee," she said, rubbing her eyes. "You know my old eyes don't work before noon. Read it to me, honey."

Mamaw does that a lot. Tricks me into reading. Like when the mail comes or we're at the grocery store.

Maybe Mamaw needs glasses.

"Well, it says 'Today our class is going on a boring trip to pick some wormy apples and you need to sign this or, like, Trevor Lee can't go.'" I pretended to point to each word as I read.

"That's exactly what it says?" asked Mamaw.

"Egg… zactly."

"Mercy. Then who am I to stand in your way of picking some wormy apples. Hand me a pen."

Mamaw wrote her name. Real slow like. It looked like a big ole scribble.

I didn't care.

At least we wouldn't be in school today. Lucky for us 3rd Graders. The kindergarten kids used to go on the Apple Picking trip. That is, until the great Apple Picking Disaster of '02. Just as the kids were gathered under the apple trees, a big wind blew by. Falling apples knocked out over a dozen kids. At least half of the class had concussions.

A concussion is when you get hit on the head and your head spins. And you think you're a cucumber or something. For a little while anyway. And you can't go to sleep or you'll never wake up. Not even if you smell bacon frying in the kitchen. Not even for your birthday. It's like serious.

With my permission slip in hand, I boarded the bus. Pinky was already saving me a seat. In the back. Those are the seats that send you rocketing into the air.

"To the moon!" Pinky likes to yell with each bump. He thinks he's an astronaut. That's why he's my best friend.

"Look," Pinky said. "I wore my pants with extra pockets. Pockets in the front. Pockets in the back. And lots of pockets on the side. He pointed to each pocket as he introduced it.

"We can stuff apples in every one of them. And no one will see."

"Smart thinking," I added. "I'll probably eat like seventeen. How many you gonna eat?" I asked.

"Mother gave me such a big breakfast, as if I was going away for a week. So, I'll probably only be able to eat like a hundred," Pinky answered.

He was serious.

He might be small, but Mamaw—who knows a lot about such things—says he can eat his weight in biscuits.

The Boog collected our permission slips. Gave us a speech about how to behave in public. How we represented her. Ourselves. Our families. Our school. Our state. Our street. And our country. Jeez-Louise.

Then off we went.

To keep us from fooling around, The Boog started rattling off math word problems. Instead of singing a roadtrip song or something fun like that. I mean, really? Bus time means "teacher zip-it" time. Everyone knows that.

"If we have 20 students," The Boog said. Even though we were ALL giving her the stink eye. "And each student fills one basket of apples today. How many baskets will we fill up?" Then she smiled like she was excited to know the answer. Cause she didn't really know it. Or, she thought she was doing a good teacher job. By bugging us during our bus trip.

"18," shouted Pinky.

Everyone giggled. Sally May and Sally Fay

giggled the loudest.

"How did you arrive at your answer?" asked The Boog. In her official "I'm being a good teacher" voice.

"Cause me and Trevor Lee will eat all the apples in our baskets," he announced.

The Boog's face melted from friendly to fierce. "Let me remind you all of something," she announced. Then she reviewed the three rules for the trip. The ones about throwing apples, picking them up from the ground, and not using ladders. And she added a fourth: NO Eating Apples.

"I encourage you to remember these rules throughout the day," she said. And stared right at Pinky. Her left eyeball twitching.

We both knew what "encourage" means. It is when someone wants you to do something because that's what they would do. But you really don't have to do it.

Mother encourages me to not cut my own hair. Daddy encourages me to stop baptizing the cat. But I think "no, no way, never gonna happen."

Encourage makes adults feel like they're doing their job. Without being too bossy.

"I feel very encouraged ma'am," said Pinky. And smiled.

That shut The Boog up. She plopped down in her seat. Quiet like a good teacher should be on a bus trip. And stared at the road.

I knew these roads like a cow knows how to moo. It only took a few minutes before the first bump.

"Here it comes," I warned Pinky.

"To the moon!" he yelled as we flew into the air.

Sally May and Sally Fay turned and gave us a look.

I waved on the way down.

"Here comes another one," I warned again.

"Wheeeeeee!" That was a big one. My hair practically touched the bus ceiling.

"You boys need to settle down," sneered Sally

May.

"Yeah. Or we're gonna tell Miss Burger," added Sally Fay.

"Well, if you had your brooms you could fly with us," laughed Pinky, grabbing his belly.

"Hey Buddy," I said. "You look a little funny. Do you feel okay?"

"I just think my breakfast is swimming around in my stomach. That's all," he said.

"Okay, buddy. Cause here comes the biggest bump of all."

We both pretended to put on our helmets. Hands in air. Ready to fly.

Maybe the bus was going a bit too fast. Or maybe Pinky should have eaten a smaller breakfast. Cause, on the way up everything seemed fine.

But on the way down.

Pinky's biscuits, eggs, sausage, pancakes, fried potatoes, muffins, toaster treats, and gravy found a new plate. On top of Sally May and Sally Fay.

We were thirty minutes late to the apple farm.

Miss Burger had to hose down the twins.

And, Pinky had to sit in the front seat for the rest of the trip.

Next to The Boog!

Some days a boy just shouldn't get out of bed.

Chapter 8⅛

Sitting in the back of the bus alone gave me time to think. Going over all these hills reminded me of another trip I had taken. In the 2nd Grade. Me, Pinky, and our parents went by bus to a nearby amusement park. Dollywood. Created by the famous country singer Dolly Parton.

A giant billboard with her picture on it welcomed us to the park.

"Now that's a singer with a big voice," said Daddy. He couldn't stop staring at her. Said he really, really liked her big voice. The biggest voice he ever did see. Mother smacked him on the arm. I'm not sure why. It was just a friendly compliment.

After buying our tickets, we raced to the Rivertown Junction. And hopped on the Smoky Mountain River Rampage. Sure to get you soaked by the end. Our parents put on raincoats, but me and Pinky went for the full drench. "Drowned rats" Daddy called us.

After that we rode the Tennessee Tornado and the Thunderbird roller coasters. Pinky waved his hands above his head as we dipped and spun and twisted and turned. I held on to the little bar so tight my fingers were curled for the rest of the day. And only opened my eyes once or twice. But it was real fun.

It was lunchtime when we finally took a break.

"My feet are killing me," said Mother. Everyone agreed it was time to sit for a spell. But where?

We narrowed it down to the *Sit and Sip* or *Miss Lillian's Chicken House*. The chickens won.

An older lady dressed in a flowered dress and straw hat and carrying a banjo danced around out front. She made up a song about Pinky's hair. And waved a rubber chicken around. I liked this crazy chicken lady. *The food here must be great*, I thought.

Posted at the entrance was an over-sized menu. Pinky began reading it. I just looked at the pictures at the bottom. The drinks.

"What'll you have boys?" asked Daddy.

"Oh look," said Pinky. "They have brown sugar cinnamon apples!"

"What else?" I asked. "I wasn't in an apple mood."

"Now read the menu on your own, Trevor Lee," said Mother. "Decide which meat you want. There are several listed that you like."

I pointed above the drinks and pretended like I was reading.

"Not there," said Daddy. "Can't you find it?"

Pinky leaned in and put his finger at the top. Where the meats were listed. "Baked chicken. Fried chicken. Chicken fried steak. And Miss Lillian's special of the day," he read. "I hope the special is a hot dog!"

It was then that Mother and Daddy heard how well Pinky read.

And saw that I couldn't.

They looked sad. Like when your favorite singer doesn't win the talent show. And you called twenty times to vote for him.

I was relieved Pinky stepped in to help me that day. And he's been stepping in ever since. It never bothers him one bit. That's why he's my best friend.

And that's why I still haven't been able to tell him that I might get sent back to 2nd Grade. Sitting in the half-empty seat. Without Pinky. That must be what it would feel like. Or worse.

Some days are as bad as an amusement park with broken-down rides.

Chapter 9

I got to team up with Pinky once we got off the bus at the apple farm. The farm was owned by the Saw family and was the biggest apple orchard in the county.

Instead of calling it Saw's Apples or Saw's Really Big Apple Orchard That's the Biggest You'll Ever Ever See, they named it Apple Saw's.

The Boog thought that was funny.

Old people have weird jokes.

Mr. Saw took us on a tour of the orchard. We watched the big machines that clean and sort the apples. We learned how they make apple pie, applesauce, and my favorite—caramel apples.

Then Mrs. Saw gave each of us a little basket. Our job was to fill the basket with the best apples we could find. They would sell some of the apples to their customers in their store. And ship the rest to nearby stores. In return, we would each get two shiny, red apples.

That's how she said it. Two shiny, red apples. Like she was in a commercial.

"Excuse me, ma'am," I said. "Is that considered minimum wage for all the work we'll be doing for you?"

I knew all about getting paid for work. Mother and Daddy gave me a dollar each week for not falling asleep in church. I've earned three dollars so far this year. It's only September, so I'm on a roll.

Before Mrs. Saw could answer, The Boog thanked her for the tour and letting us visit the farm. Then whisked us out the door to begin our apple picking.

Pinky took off running. That kid is like a cheetah. I chased after him until he stopped. At the last tree.

"No one will bug us here," he said.

"Good thinking!"

"Yeah. We can throw, bite, and smash all the apples we want."

Pinky is always good at remembering which rule he wants to break first.

"Maybe we should fill our buckets. Real fast like. Get it over with."

"Uh… sure," said Pinky. And he rolled his eyes.

So we looked under the tree. We found apples with spots. Apples with bruises. Apples with bite marks. And apples with worms. But no "shiny, red" apples like Mrs. Saw said she needed.

"Well, it looks like we're in a heap of applesauce with no spoon," I said. "We can't go back with these apples in our buckets."

"We'll have to take to the sky," responded Pinky.

"What? Haven't you flown enough for one day?"

"I mean we'll have to climb," said Pinky.

"How?" I asked. I wasn't quite the skinny

mini that Pinky was. I was more of a land-based mammal.

"Well, we'll have to use a ladder," thought Pinky out loud.

Now this is the moment I should have remembered Rule #2 on the instruction sheet. No climbing ladders. But instead…

"Hey," I said pointing. "There's one over there by the tractor."

Pinky and I dragged the ladder to the tree.

"This ladder looks like it has seen ten miles of bad road," I said. "Are you sure it'll hold me?"

"Just step lightly," said Pinky.

"Good idea. Think small."

Pinky crawled up the ladder first. He was faster than his parents leaving the house on Date Night.

"Hey!" he yelled. "Get a look at this."

Pinky tossed down a shiny, red apple into his bucket.

"Two points!" I clapped.

"Come on up," he said. "The picking's mighty fine up here."

So, like a fish swimming into the mouth of a whale... I went.

Step over step. Step over step.

Or should I say creak over creak.

With each step the ladder seem to sag. Kinda like an over-filled baby diaper.

"Are you really sure this ladder will hold me?" I asked. And as soon as I did the loudest creak I ever did hear rang throughout the orchard.

"Grab the tree limb!" yelled Pinky.

I did with one hand just as the ladder cracked

in two and fell to the ground.

Pinky tugged and pulled the other hand. And tugged and pulled some more.

I grunted and groaned. And grunted and groaned. And then just groaned.

Finally I wedged myself between two limbs.

"We did it!" smiled Pinky.

Yeah, we did it all right.

"Uh, Pinky?" I asked. "It's a great view and all from up here. But, how we gonna get down?"

Pinky looked at me. And I looked at Pinky.

"HELP!"

Some days are worse than a rotten wormy apple.

Chapter 10

It's a good thing Pinky is the loudest kid in the class. Soon, everyone came a running. The Saws had to call the fire department to get us down. The whole class thought it was real cool when they heard the sirens and saw the fire truck.

"That'll be me someday," smiled Pinky as he pointed to the truck.

The firemen had a long, metal ladder. It would get us down. Although I wasn't sure I wanted back on the ground. Not with The Boog a whoopin' and a hollerin' the way she was.

But, The Boog stopped yelling when the firemen showed up. In fact, I never in all my life heard a teacher giggle so much. I'll have to ask her what's so funny about firemen. Maybe, it's their plastic pants? You wouldn't catch me dead wearing plastic pants! Not even if I wet the bed for a whole year.

On the bus ride back to school, Pinky sat on one side of The Boog. I sat on the other. She smelled real nice. Like apples and sweat.

It made me a bit hungry.

That's cause we didn't get our two shiny, red apples. So unfair.

The Boog made us write twenty times "I will not break the apple picking rules." I thought that was kinda stupid since we were never going apple picking again.

I told her, too. "I think this is kinda stupid since we won't never go apple picking again. Maybe it would be better if we weren't allowed to ever be line leader or read on Family Night. Now that would be bad. Real bad." And I made my best sad face.

The Boog popped an aspirin and told me to

keep writing. She really needs to comb her hair.

And as we fled off the school bus, The Boog yelled one last thing… "Don't forget Monday is Picture Day!"

Some days are as bad as a yo-yo with no string.

Chapter 10½

I forgot.

It took only three steps for it to completely dissolve in my brain. Only the important things stick. Like the five uses for a ruler. (One involves measuring. The other four might get you into trouble.) And how to race turtles in the toilet without getting caught.

But who cares. It was the weekend. And Pinky was coming over to stay.

When we burst through the front door, Daddy was already home.

"Anything exciting happen at school today?" he asked.

"No. What have you heard?" me and Pinky said together. "And why are you already home?"

"Half day at work," said Daddy. "My favorite kind of day."

But before he could ask again about our day, we tossed our bookbags on the floor. And headed back out the door.

"We're gonna go the barn," I yelled.

"Well, check to see if your Mamaw needs anything first. She's in the kitchen."

We stopped in our tracks and made a quick side trip.

"Hey sweetpea," Mamaw said as she saw us. And gave me a big squeeze.

"And you too sweetpea junior," she laughed. And hugged Pinky. Shaking her itchy head.

"Do you need any help before me and Pinky go play in the barn?" I asked.

"How about you see if I missed any eggs in the coop this morning? I'm baking a cake for tonight and need a few extra. If not, I'll have to run to the store."

"Sure," I said. "With Pinky by my side Hippie is sure to keep his distance."

Hippie was no different from your average person. Anyone who had run into Pinky either liked him, or kept their distance. Hippie chose the latter.

When we headed out to the coop, Hippie was nowhere in sight.

"Maybe he ran back into the woods," said Pinky. "Or is taking a nap."

I didn't much care where he was. As long as he stayed away from me.

When we reached the coop, I grabbed the door and swung it open.

There stood Hippie. On guard.

I let out a scream that caused the hens to fly off their nests, scampering to the back of the coop. Quickly, I slammed the door shut.

"We'll just tell your Mamaw there weren't any eggs," said Pinky.

I nodded and tried to catch my breath.

Mamaw let us ride with her to the store. Even gave each of us a quarter for the gum machines.

At the front door someone had stacked small

bags of apples. From the Saw's apple orchard.

"Do y'all want me to get a bag to make a pie this weekend?" Mamaw asked. "I already used up the ones I picked the other day."

"No ma'am," I said. Pinky's eyes got big like he was having a nightmare flashback. I grabbed his arm and walked him into the store.

We didn't make eye contact with the apples on the way out either. But I could tell they were looking at us.

Once home, Mamaw let us help her bake the cake. I got to do all the measuring. A ½ cup of this and a ½ cup of that. Then we both got to lick the mixing bowl and spoon. There was nothing better than Mamaw's chocolate chip cake with chocolate icing.

And the best part about it was we got to eat the first slices. Since Mother and

Daddy left for Date Night before the cake was finished. They were going bowling with Pinky's parents.

After cake, Mamaw popped us a big bowl of popcorn and we plopped in front of the TV. To watch *Horror on 83rd Street*. My favorite scary movie. I still jumped and screamed at every scary part. Not Mamaw. She sat there like a stone. "It ain't real," she said. "No need to get all worked up over it."

I'm not sure when we fell asleep, but we woke up the next morning. On the floor. With Barks-a-Lot licking our faces. Mamaw was in the kitchen making a pan of biscuits. And frying up some sweet-smelling bacon.

"How you taking your eggs this morning, boys?" she asked.

"Scrambled for me," I mumbled as I stumbled into the kitchen.

"Ditto," said Pinky.

As we gobbled down breakfast, the phone rang. Mother answered.

"Uh-huh," she said. "I see. Uh-huh. Oh, dear."
She looked at me. Then she looked at Pinky.

"Pinky, you mother needs to speak to you on the phone," she announced. "Seems like she ran into Miss Burger this morning at the grocery store."

"Tell her I'm not here," whispered Pinky.

There was a noise on the other end of the phone.

"She says come to the phone or come home."

Pinky moped over to the phone and reluctantly put it to his ear. Mother walked over to me and said, "We'll talk about this later."

Boy did Pinky get an earful. His face turned pink. Then red. Then splotchy. Then redder. Then white.

"Yes, ma'am," was all he said as he put the phone down.

"Looks like we best be staying out of your Mother's hair today," said Daddy as he leaned in. "How about I take you boys fishing down by the creek?"

It took us 36 seconds to finish eating, put on our play clothes, and storm out the door. Daddy collected the poles. And gave us a big empty coffee can to put some worms in. It wasn't too hard finding some. What with the rain last night. The worms we collected wiggled and squiggled at the bottom of the can. With no idea they were about to be fish food.

It didn't take us long to get to the creek and get set up. Daddy prepared the fishing rods. "Let's see," he said. As he peered down into the worm-filled coffee can. "It looks like there are at least three worms for each of us."

"That's three times three," I said. "So, that makes… ." And I stared right at Daddy. Wondering if he really could multiply.

"Nine," blurted Pinky. "You know that."

I gave Pinky my "you be quiet" look. But he didn't understand it. He

doesn't really know what "be quiet" means anyway.

"You're right," said Daddy. "Three times three is nine. Now enough math for today."

I smiled.

Mamaw was right.

We returned home just in time for dinner. After that, me and Pinky each got a clear canning jar and ran outside to catch lightning bugs.

"If we fill up the jar," Pinky said. "We'll have a night light that will last for a week."

"Yeah, but Mother always makes me let the lightning bugs go after a day. She says it's not right to keep them caged up. Animals with wings need to fly."

"Whatever," said Pinky. And started snatching lightning bugs from the evening sky.

Once we caught enough, we sat on the back porch. And admired our trophies. This day couldn't get any better.

"So," said Pinky. "Are you all practiced for your Family Night part?"

Boom.

Why did he have to bring that up now?

"Actually, I have something to tell you," I said.

"You're in love with The Boog?" Pinky laughed.

"Shut up!" I yelled.

"No you shut up," said Pinky. And pushed me off the porch.

When I climbed back up I knew I had to tell him the truth. He was my best friend after all.

"Pinky," I said. "If I don't do well on the reading, Mother and Daddy are going to talk to The Boog about putting me back in 2nd Grade."

Pinky sat there real quiet for a while. When he spoke, it was slow and sure.

"No they won't," he said. "I have a plan.

The next morning, Pinky sprung out of bed with a twinkle in his eye. He was a boy on a mission. And I liked it.

"So, did you hear about Miss Owens?" asked Pinky. As we all got in the car to go to church. "You know, the 2nd Grade teacher. I hear she's gone crazy. Even bit a couple students. Everyone's getting tested for rabies. That 2nd Grade sure isn't a safe place for a kid." Then he looked at me and smiled.

"Yeah," I said. "I hear all the kids crying every time I go by her classroom." This fib was getting off to a good start.

"You did?" asked Mother.

"Yes," we both said together. And shook our heads up and down so hard it started to hurt.

"That's odd," said Mother. "I saw Miss Owens at the grocery store last week. She's been at home with her new baby for months. But she says she's coming back to school at the end of the month. She's such a sweet lady."

Me and Pinky looked at each other.

Our parents really needed to start shopping at another store. One where teachers weren't allowed.

We spent the rest of the trip in silence.

At church, I told Pinky that Mother and Daddy paid me a dollar if I stayed awake. I'd split it with him if he helped me. But he fell asleep before we finished singing the second song. I was gone before the preacher started.

After church, Mother and Daddy said we could stop and get ice cream before dropping Pinky off at his house. We each got two scoops of chocolate. With sprinkles. Then it was off to Pinky's.

"You have all your stuff?" asked Mother. As we pulled into the driveway.

"Yes, ma'am," Pinky said.

"I hope you had fun this weekend," said Daddy.

"I certainly did," said Pinky. "Next weekend, it's my house."

"Can I go?" I asked Mother.

"Only if it's okay with his parents. You call us later Pinky and let us know."

"See you at school," Pinky waved as he hopped out of the car. "Don't forget tomorrow is Picture Day."

Some days aren't half bad,
but there's nothing better
than a whole weekend
with your best friend.

Chapter 11

I forgot.

Again.

Like I told you. Only the important things stick.

Not only did I wear something old. It was dirty. And smelled like chicken fingers and mustard. My stomach growled. But, you can't smell a shirt in a picture, so who cares.

We all lined up and marched to the gym. Bobby Sue, the line leader, led the way. Pinky and I held up the rear until we got to the gym. That's where the almost bald guy with the camera sat. The Boog told us that one at a time we had to sit in front of this big, blue screen. Then 1, 2, 3 the almost hairless man would snap our picture.

She said it was important that we smile real big like. That's cause these pictures would be shown next to our color poems on Family Night. The Boog was also gonna make a slideshow out of them for our "special" reading.

Smile. Now this was something I could do. No reading required. But, I wondered what kind of smile I should do to go next to my poem. How does one smile for chicken doo-doo? A big toothy smile? Or lips closed with a wink of the eye?

Just thinking about Family Night made my stomach feel like it had butterflies in it. And lizards chasing the butterflies. And sharks chasing the lizards. And a dinosaur chasing them all.

"It's a good thing your mom left your hair alone this year," I whispered to Pinky. Trying to forget about Family Night and reading.

"Yeah. Daddy said she learned her lesson. She didn't even get a time-out or nothin' for it."

"Here you go boys," said The Boog. She handed each of us a little black comb. And continued on down the line.

"What are we supposed to do with these?" I asked.

Sally May turned around. Her hands on her hips. "You boys are animals! Don't you even know how to comb your hair?"

"Moo," said Pinky.

"Cock-a-doodle-doo," I added.

"You two look like you just rolled out of bed," said Sally Fay. "Miss Burger!"

The Boog gave us her "stink eye" teacher look. Pinky began acting like he was combing his hair.

"Ain't I pretty," he laughed.

"It's your turn, Trevor Lee," interrupted The Boog.

The man behind the camera began to bark directions. With each direction the few strands of hair on his head flipped from one side to the other. I watched like you'd watch a tennis match.

"Sit straight."

"Turn your legs to the side."

"No, the other side."

"Smile."

"Stop moving your head, son."

"Wait. Comb your hair on the left. It's sticking out."

"Relax, young man."

I stopped and gave him my "don't be dumb" look and… snap! The picture was taken.

Mother was gonna like this one.

Then the camera man lined the whole class up. In three rows. One behind the other.

Pinky and I darted to the back row.

"I can't see you Pinky," said The Boog. "You'll need to move up front."

Pinky hated the front row. It reminded him that he was the shortest kid in the whole entire class.

"We can hold him up," I offered. I grabbed under Pinky's right arm. Elmer grabbed under his left. And we lifted him up. Now he was as tall as we were.

1, 2, 3… snap! Elmer's arm gave out right when the almost baldy man took the picture. Pinky dove forward. The front row fell like dominoes. Not the pizza. The little black cubes with dots.

Sally May's dress flew up over her head. She was wearing underwear with Sunday written on it. And it was already Monday! Sally Fay rolled out into The Boog and knocked her down.

"Just one day," muttered The Boog, as she

pulled herself up. "I only ask for one day."

She looked up into the ceiling as she spoke.
Then she got real mad. Like she finally saw those
brown spots. And grizzly-looking dead flies. "Just
get in your lines and no moving. Is that clear?"
she screamed.

"Clear as mud," I whispered to Pinky. "Clear…
as… mud."

Then she walked over to the corner and took a little something from her purse while we got back in our lines.

Some days a teacher feels
like a cow with the runs.

Chapter 12

I thought Picture Day couldn't get any worse. But it did.

When we got back to the room, a note for The Boog stuck to the door.

The Boog had a look on her face like the time last week Pinky put a pencil in his nose and the eraser got stuck. He was afraid to take it out because he thought it would erase his memory. The Boog tried to tell him it didn't work that way. But he wasn't convinced. It wasn't until I told him there wasn't anything worth remembering that he let her pull it out.

"I have some bad news," said The Boog as we took our seats. "It looks like Walter has the chicken pox."

"Wow! I didn't even know Walter had chickens," I said. That's cause Walter lives in an apartment. Chickens in an apartment are way cool!

"Hey," whispered Pinky. "You have chickens. Maybe you can get that pox thingy."

"Does it hurt?" I asked.

"I think it's a little itchy. That's all. You get these red marks all over your face. Like fat freckles."

Fat freckles. I could handle that. Pinky is a genius. Things were sure looking up for me!

The Boog went on. "So, he won't be able to read his part on Family Night tomorrow." "Oh, no! This is a DI-SAS-TER!" cried out Sally May and Sally Fay at the same time. "Walter is our best reader. And, he has the longest part."

"Well, that means I will need to divide up his part and assign it to some of you," said The Boog. She's a quick thinker, too.

Then she paused and looked at me. I ducked under my desk. I'm a quicker thinker.

I had the end of the story. There was no way I was going to get stuck with the beginning. That was the hardest part of all. That's when everyone is paying attention. By the end, half of them will be snoring. So, no one will hear me read.

"Trevor Lee," The Boog said.

"Trevor Lee isn't here today," I announced in a deep voice from under the desk. Like the kind you hear in a scary movie.

Then Pinky jumped in. "Trevor Lee is in the bathroom, ma'am."

That's why he's my best friend.

"Trevor Lee," The Boog said once more, now standing over my desk. I could see her toes poking out of her shoes. Like hawk claws. That lady needs to clip her toenails.

"I need you to read the first paragraph of the story."

Uh-oh!

I've sure been through a lot of uh-oh's since school started this year. But this was the biggest uh-oh in the history of uh-oh's.

Earth swallow me now.

I crawled out from under my desk.

"Just checking for ticks and fleas, ma'am," I smiled. "How many words is that first paragraph you're talking about?" I asked. "Cause if I read more than like two words, I get that laryngitis stuff and can't talk no more. You wouldn't want that on your conscience now would you?"

"It's three short sentences," answered The Boog. "We can work on it during recess."

Recess? Work? What did I do to deserve this punishment?

Well, okay. Don't answer that.

But still!

I couldn't read three whole sentences. In front of the entire universe and their Mamaws.

Some days a boy should
just dig a hole to China.
And never come back.

Chapter 13

The number 13 is unlucky. About as unlucky as I am now. So, I'm not about to write anything in this chapter. Turn the page.

And fast.

No, faster than that.

Even faster. Hurry!

And don't look back.

Chapter 14

That's better.

So, where were we?

Oh, right. My life was about to end.

Not only did I have to read the first paragraph on Family Night, but The Boog made me stay in for recess to practice.

We went through every word. One cotton pickin' letter at a time. The Boog helped me sound out each one.

"This letter stands for the 'sssss' sound," she said. I hissed and looked at her for another clue. "And it rhymes with 'goop'."

"Snoop?" I asked.

"No, look closer at the letters and don't add any extra sounds," The Boog reminded me.

"Sssss… oop. What's the word?"

"Soup!" I yelled. Yikes. This was gonna be harder than the time I taught my goldfish to dance.

After that doozie of a word, I crept on to the next one. Then the next. And so on. But, before I got to the end of the sentence, I forgot where I started. This made no sense.

These sentences were much longer than The Boog had said. I think she's a big fibber. That's a nice way of saying "liar, liar, The Boog's pants were on fire."

Teachers aren't supposed to do that, you know. Unless they're meeting with your parents and you did something really bad. Then they can tell a lie as big as the whole continent of South Africa.

"I'll never be able to do this," I sighed.

"I believe in you, Trevor Lee," she whispered. Then, The Boog put her hand on my shoulder. And I didn't even mind.

When I got home that night, Mamaw was waiting for me with a big biscuit. Filled with strawberry jelly.

"What happened to you?" she asked. "It looks like a bear stole your grin."

I told Mamaw about my terrible, horrible, no good, very bad, awful, disastrous day.

"It'll take a lot of practice," said Mamaw. "But you can do it. Why don't you read it to me?"

I started the way The Boog had told me. "Once upon a... ."

Then I stopped.

"What's that word?" I asked Mamaw. But she didn't even look at the book.

"Trevor Lee, your teacher would want you to do it yourself. That's how you'll learn."

I looked at each letter. Remembered what sound The Boog said it made. Then put them altogether.

"Once upon a time," I said. "Well, that only took half an hour. It'll be midnight before I get through this sentence. And next week before I get through this paragraph." I covered my face with my hands. Not because I was crying or nothing

like that you know.

"Just take your time, honey," said Mamaw.
"You'll get it."

All evening I practiced reading those three
mile-long sentences. I read them to Mamaw.
I read them to Barks-A-Lot. Who just snored
through the whole thing. I even read them to
the hens. After I raced Hippie the Rooster to the
chicken coop, of course.

The hens were the best audience. They
gathered around and clucked after each sentence.

One even laid an egg to show me how much she liked it. I think a couple rolled their eyes when I messed up, though. I'll remember those hens the next time Mamaw wants to make fried chicken for dinner.

While sitting in the chicken coop an idea popped into my head. And it only hurt a little.

I really could get the chicken pox just like Pinky had suggested, I thought. Maybe even the small pox. I had also heard of that. But this was a serious problem. So I should probably try to get the large pox. That would be a sure-fire way to get me out of Family Night. And I was sure my chickens had the chicken pox, the small pox, AND the large pox. Don't all chickens?

Mamaw says you can get sick easy-like from someone else who is sick. For starters, she says you can get sick if you shake hands with someone who is sick. You can also get sick if they sneeze or cough on you. Or if you kiss them. It was worth a shot. I mean, worth a try. It's one thing getting sick. It's another thing getting a shot.

So, I began shaking hands with the chickens. "How do you do?" I asked. Most of the ones I could snatch pulled away and raced to the back of the coop as soon as I tried to clutch their claws. A couple tried to peck my hand off.

I wasn't sure that was going to work, so I considered the next way to get sick—cough or sneeze. But how do you make a chicken sneeze? I could throw pepper into the air. That always made me sneeze.

There was no pepper around, so I threw some of the chicken feed up in the air. I immediately began sneezing like a tornado was shooting out of my nose. The chickens started clucking and squawking and flying around to grab the seeds as they fell to the ground. It was like a bunch of old ladies at Walmart fighting over the 90% off sale bin. And I didn't hear even one chicken sneeze in all the mess.

The last way to get sick was to kiss one of the chickens.

Never gonna happen.

Not even with Veronica.

I just had to hope that my hand shaking did the trick. Surely by morning I would be as itchy as a bee sting on your butt.

When Mother and Daddy got home, I read to them, too. I didn't want them to get the pox thingy, so I kept my distance.

Daddy watched the baseball game on TV while I read to him. "Almost there," he said. "Keep practicing."

Mother checked her emails while I read to her. "Almost there," she said. "Keep practicing."

Mamaw brought me a big bowl of ice cream. With caramel sauce.

"You need your energy for all that practicing," she said. Then she winked at me.

This reading stuff was more exhausting than running uphill backwards while being chased by an angry goose.

Don't ask.

And, I only had one day before Family Night.

I wonder how fast you can catch the chicken pox? Or malaria?

Some days lay a big rotten egg.

Chapter 15

When the alarm clock went off I rolled over and yelled "Liar!" Then I rolled back and went to sleep. Mamaw had to shake the covers to get me out of bed.

"So today is the day," I grumbled. Rubbing my eyes. "The soon-to-be worst day of my life."

Unless...

I sat up in bed. A little too fast. And spilled onto the floor. I pulled myself up and thrust my face into the mirror.

"Do you see these red spots?" I asked Mamaw. "I think I have the pox."

Mamaw ran over. Held my face in her hands. And leaned in real close.

"Honey, those are just your freckles," she said.

And took a deep breath.

"Are you sure?" I asked. "They look a little fatter than usual to me. Like those chicken pox things."

"Sweetpea, you're as healthy as a diet candy bar," she said. And went downstairs to finish cooking breakfast.

"Those chickens can't do anything right," I grumbled. "All I wanted was a little disease. Was that too much to ask for?"

At school The Boog had on a fancy, new dress. With big flowers and buttons the size of Pinky's head. And her hair was all curly. She even had some red stuff on her lips and cheeks. She cleans up real nice. For a girl.

"Let's go down to the gym and practice reading our story," she said. "It'll be just like we'll do it tonight."

We all lined up like sardines in one of those stinky silver cans. The kind with a pull-tab and lots of juice.

"Smile," said The Boog. "And hold your books

up high."

I put mine over my head.

"A little lower please, Trevor Lee."

Well, she said "high." You heard it.

"Now, I will count to three very softly. When I finish, I want everyone to say the name of the story together. Let's practice. 1... 2... 3."

"The name of the story together," we all said.

"No!" said The Boog, her hands shaking. "Read the title of the story. Let's try again. 1... 2... 3."

"The... the . .. little... red . .. little... the... hen. Hen."

"Let's try that one more time," said The Boog. A big drop of sweat rolled down her forehead and onto her face. It left a white strip down the middle of the red circle on her cheek.

"I will say it slowly and you say it with me."

We did that about a thousand hundred times before The Boog said it was right.

"Now, as soon as we say the title of the story, Trevor Lee will begin reading. Nice and loud."

The room went silent.

This was the moment.

The Boog held her breath.

Pinky held his breath.

Sally May, Sally Fay, Walter, and the rest of the class held their breath.

Even I held my breath.

Which is like really hard when you're supposed to read.

"I told you he couldn't read," whispered Sally May. This is why she's still my Enemy #1.

"You can do it," said The Boog. "Take a deep breath and do it like we practiced."

Take a deep breath? I haven't breathed since last week.

"Once upon a… time," I whispered.

"Louder," said The Boog. "Say it like you're talking to the person in the last row. Or, talking to Pinky out for recess."

"ONCE UPON A TIME," I yelled.

"Keep going," smiled The Boog.

I got through the first sentence. Took another

wheezy breath. Then the second. I needed help on three of the bigger words. And finally the third. I messed up a little on that one, too.

After that I just stared at the ceiling until the end. I didn't even care that it had brown spots. And dead flies. I just had to be perfect tonight. But I wasn't even close yet.

Some days are longer than a ten-word sentence.

Chapter 15½

The Boog reminded us to return to school at 7 o'clock sharp. Told us to practice our parts one last time at home. Try to eat a hearty dinner. And wear something "worthy of the stage." Whatever that meant.

I had three types of clothes. School clothes. Church clothes. And play clothes. But no stage clothes. Maybe The Boog meant we should dress like a character in a play. Such as a frog prince. Or a troll. I did have an ugly green shirt Mother bought me.

When I got home, Mamaw had sloppy joes simmering on the stove. And tater tots crisping in the oven. My favorite.

"What's eating you up, sweetpea?" she asked.

As she fixed me a plate.

Mother and Daddy glanced at each other. And got quiet. I could tell their stomachs were as flip-floppy as mine.

"I have a headache. That's all," I said. "I think all that practice reading today gave me brain damage. My head's swollen. Real bad."

"You'll kick this reading thing in the butt tonight," said Daddy. "Don't worry." And he gave me a high five. But it felt more like a low three. "Sometimes it takes a little extra time to get it right," he went on. "It took your Mother years of practice before I could eat her cooking."

"Ain't that the truth," whispered Mamaw.

"But we're proud of you for working so hard," said Mother, ignoring them. "And if you need more help, we'll talk to Miss Burger. About some other solution."

Other solution?

We all knew what that meant. 2nd Grade. And if I didn't read well tonight, that was exactly where I was going to end up.

I popped a tater tot into my mouth. And swirled it around. But it just wouldn't go down.

I stared at my plate. *The life of a tater tot is so easy*, I thought. It starts out as a spud. Grows up to be a big, fat potato. Then gets made into the best thing possible. A tot. No problems. No worries. No Family Night.

I couldn't eat another bite.

Mamaw patted my hand. "Why don't you go upstairs and take a nap," she suggested. "I'll wrap up a sloppy joe for you to eat later."

I trudged up to my room. Fell on top of the covers. And tossed. And turned. And swiveled. And swooped. Until I finally felt myself drift off to sleep.

I woke up in what looked like our field. In back of the barn. I was surrounded by our animals. Sort of. There were cows, but with big polka-dots. Chickens, but ones wearing boots. And a large gray horse who was sporting a baseball cap and a dress with extra large buttons.

"What's drooping your face?" asked the gray horse.

"It's his turn to read," clucked the chickens.

"But he doesn't know how," laughed the cows.

"We shall see," said the gray horse. And she handed me a book. 2½ feet wide and 3½ feet tall.

"Read this," said the gray horse. "But if you can't read it, you must live in the barn. Alone. Forever."

"And no visits from your best friend, Pink-eye" added the chickens.

I grabbed the book cover with both hands. Lifted the corner. And swung it open to page 3. The first page in the story.

The page had markings all over it. Like letters. Only I had never seen any of them before.

"Once upon a time?" I said. But it was really more of a question.

"No," said the gray horse. And she shook her head.

"See, he can't read," clucked the chickens.

"Send him to the barn. Forever!" said the cows.

"No!" I cried.

"Then read," said the gray horse.

"Read," said the chickens.

"READ!" yelled the cows with polka dots. And started chasing me around the field.

"AAAAAAAGGGGGGHHHHHHHHH!"

Something grabbed me by the arm. And began pulling and shaking me.

"Stop!" I cried. "I can't. I can't."

"Trevor Lee," shouted a familiar voice. "Wake up."

It was Mamaw. "You're having one fit of a dream, honey," she said. And smoothed the hair down on my face.

I rubbed my eyes. And slowly looked around.

No field. No polka-dotted cows. No laughing chickens.

It was only a dream. A nightmare. Just like tonight was going to be.

Some days you feel like
a tater tot under
a fat man's boot.

Chapter 16

7 o'clock came faster than Superman in a hurry. Everyone's parents poured into the gym and took their seats. Most were dressed in their Sunday best.

The Boog gave us our final instructions. She was talking real fast. Like she had to go to the bathroom real bad.

Then she practiced my part with me one last time.

The slideshow of our school photos started as we lined up in front of everyone. As soon as mine came up, Daddy closed his eyes. Opened them real big. Then closed them again. Mother put her hand over her mouth. Mamaw just smiled and waved.

Principal Harris introduced us as we lined up. "Miss Burger's boys and girls. Our 3rd Grade GREATS!" And then we began.

We all said the story title like The Boog taught us.

Almost.

Then it was my part.

I took one giant deep breath. Like you do when you have a "let's hold our breath" contest with Pinky before he makes you laugh and you lose.

I looked out at the audience. Mother had her eyes closed like she was saying a prayer. Daddy was looking down at the floor. Mamaw was nodding. This was it. These next three sentences would determine whether or not I had to go back to the 2nd Grade.

Then I looked at each word in the first sentence. Remembered what The Boog told me. And read it. Not too fast. But not too slow, either. I practically had it memorized.

On the second sentence I stumbled over only

one of the longer words. But recovered and made it through the third sentence okay. After that I just stared at the floor. I didn't want to look up. I didn't want to see if Mother and Daddy were disappointed.

Sally May and Sally Fay were next. They read their part pretty good.

But not as good as Pinky.

Then Elmer, Bo, Bobby Sue, Brandy, and the rest of the class read their paragraphs.

Finally we were at the end.

I turned the page and read in a voice even louder than Pinky's... "THE END!"

Then I looked up at the audience. Mother and Daddy were smiling.

"Well, butter my butt and call me Biscuit," I yelled. "I did it!"

Everyone clapped.

Mother clapped.

Daddy clapped.

The Boog clapped.

The whole audience clapped.

That means everyone.

I looked over at Mamaw and she was a clappin' and a bawlin' at the same time.

I walked over to Mother. "Why is Mamaw crying?" I asked.

"She's happy," answered Mother.

"Happy that it's over?" I asked. "Me, too."

"No," smiled Mother. "Just happy that you read so well."

"Why?"

"Trevor Lee, honey, when your Mamaw was a little girl she had a big family. She had to take care of all her younger brothers and sisters. So, she never got to go to school."

"No school. How lucky!" I said.

"No, Trevor Lee. Since your Mamaw never went to school, she never learned to read. That's why she's so happy you can."

Then it all made sense. Mamaw wasn't always trying to trick me into reading. She needed me to read. She needed me to read
for her.

I walked over to Mamaw and opened my book.

"You see this here?" I asked. "This here is the letter 's'. It makes the 'sssss' sound. Like a scary hissy snake."

Mamaw stopped crying and said "ssss."

"And this here makes the 'uh' sound. Like you're kinda confused and can't think of what to say."

Mamaw said "uh" and looked a little confused.

Don't worry, Mamaw," I said. "I might not be great at it, but I'll try my best to teach ya to read."

"You think I can learn?" she asked.

"Yes," I said. "And I'm as sure as the sun rising in the morning."

Well, that's pretty near how that dreaded Family Night ended.

Okay. I know what you're thinking.

I admit it.

Once in a while you have a good day. Maybe even a great day. But trust me. It won't become a habit. Especially not if you're in the 3rd Grade.

But that's exactly where I planned on staying.

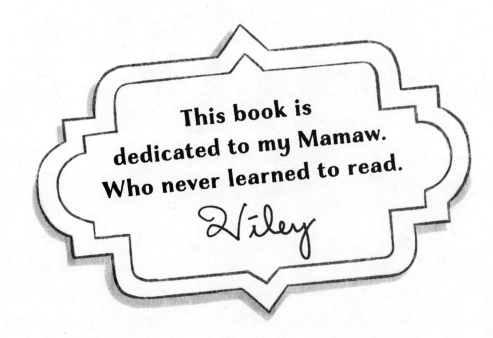

This book is dedicated to my Mamaw. Who never learned to read.

Wiley

219823192280ΘΟ